The Pony
That Kept a Secret

BY ELISABETH HUBBARD LANSING

Illustrated by Barbara Cooney

NEW YORK: THOMAS Y. CROWELL COMPANY

This is for
MISS LYD

Contents

The Meadow Pool

"EEEE-ow! Eeeee-ow!"

Ted stood on the stone wall by the drive and looked across the lawn. Where was Sue? The last time he had seen her she was going toward the barn with Robby trotting at her heels. He gave the signal once more.

A faint answering cry came from inside the barn. Ted grinned. Sue had heard him. He jumped from the wall, ran across the lawn, and plunged into the cornfield below the house. The tall stalks slashed at his legs and arms like razor blades. But Ted didn't care. He had thought of

1

a new idea and not a thing mattered but that.

He hoped Sue would hurry. Sometimes you couldn't tell about Sue. Even if she was his twin sister and ten years old like himself, she didn't always appreciate his ideas.

When Ted's signal came Sue had just settled herself in her hideaway in the hayloft. She answered him out of habit. Then she wished she hadn't. She had a new book to read and an apple to eat.

The afternoon sun slanted in the loft window and warmed the hay nest that was her hideaway. But Sue knew she must obey the signal. It was one of Ted's rules. It meant he had left a message for her in their private hiding place and she must go and read it.

As Sue put her book away a voice came from the barn floor below. It was a small voice, but high and shrill. It belonged to Robby.

"Too, Too!" cried Robby. "Wobby gotta yegg!"

A fierce cackling followed and Sue knew what Robby meant. He had disturbed the setting hen in the grain room and was taking her eggs. He

wanted Sue to see them. He called her again.

Before Sue could reply another voice joined Robby's. "Hey, young feller, none of that. That hen's settin'. Give me them eggs."

It was Pete, the hired man. Sue knew he would take care of Robby and the eggs.

She crawled over the mounds of hay and peered down over the loft. She saw Pete's bony figure bending over Robby. He was trying to tell Robby something, but Robby was roaring too loudly to hear. His round face was bright red, his yellow curls shook with anger. His mouth was wide open and the sounds that came from it rang through the barn. Robby was two years old and when he wanted something he wanted it very much.

"Pete," shrieked Sue, "try the blanket!"

Pete glanced up at Sue. His thin face with its long nose and sharp blue eyes looked desperate. He heard Sue and nodded. Then he took a little heap of cloth from the floor and stuffed it into Robby's arms. The cloth was what was left of a blanket that had once been pink. Now it was a dirty gray and torn to a tattered rag. But it was Robby's favorite thing. He carried it everywhere.

When Pete gave Robby the blanket his roars subsided. "Banka," he said and tucked it under one arm. "Wobby's yeggs."

"Wobby's yeggs nothin'," said Pete. "They're goin' back under that hen. Don't you want some baby chickens?"

Pete carried the eggs toward the grain room with Robby close at his heels. "Wobby's chickies," said Robby.

"Give her time," said Pete.

Sue waited until Robby was in the grain room

with Pete. Then she slid from the hayloft and ran to the stone wall. The hiding place was between two of the largest stones on top of the wall. Here Ted and Sue kept a pad and pencil so they could write important messages to each other. Ted had warned Sue to keep the hiding place a secret, especially from Robby.

Sue pulled out the pad and read Ted's message. "Get rid of Robby and meet me on the rock. Bring Twinkle."

Ted's writing was more scrawly than usual, so Sue knew he was excited. He must have a new idea. Ted had a great many ideas, sometimes three or four in one day.

Sue heard Robby and Pete talking in the grain room. Robby was safely out of the way for now. She ran to the barn and went quickly to Twinkle's stall.

Twinkle was a pony. He had a smooth brown coat, his mane and tail were thick and black. He held his head proudly and his ears pointed upward. Deep inside his eyes was a small bright light. That was why his name was Twinkle.

Sue flung her arms around Twinkle's neck and hugged him. Twinkle was the finest pony in the world. He had been given to the twins on their

tenth birthday. They had wished for a pony so long they sometimes couldn't believe Twinkle was really theirs.

Besides Twinkle they had a square straw cart with red seats and wheels. The cart had a little iron step behind. Twinkle had a saddle, too. It was a large felt pad with no stirrups.

As Sue saddled Twinkle she listened for sounds from the grain room above.

"Chickies quack," Robby was saying.

Sue laughed softly. Robby sounded just like a duck. Just then a real quack came from Twinkle's manger. A duck poked her head over the edge of the manger and quacked again. She sounded annoyed.

Twinkle whinnied in a soothing way. The duck and Twinkle were great friends. Twinkle had never been happy on the farm until Jemima came to live there, too. When Twinkle went out with the cart, he wouldn't move unless Jemima was placed in the cart.

"Quack," said Jemima to Twinkle. "Quack, quack, quack!" Each quack sounded angrier than the one before.

"What's the matter with you, Jemima?" said Sue, peering into the manger. "You never used to be so cross. You stay in the manger all the time now."

Jemima pecked at Sue with her flat bill.

"Whew!" cried Sue, jumping back. "You *are* cross. Never mind, Twinkle. We've got to see what Ted wants."

She climbed into the saddle and steered him into the barnyard. As she went through the gate she heard Pete say, "Go find your mother, Robby. I've got to take Chub and Nellie to the blacksmith's."

Sue sighed. Pete would let her go to the blacksmith's with him, if only she didn't have to meet Ted. It was fun to ride in the wagon behind the two big farm horses.

"Eeeee-ow!"

Ted was getting impatient. It was warm on the

big rock. The sun made the stone almost too hot to touch. His new idea would take care of the heat all right. He could hardly wait to tell Sue about it. He heard a rustling in the cornfield and gave a welcoming shout.

"Hurry up, can't you? I've been here an hour."

Sue didn't answer. She knew Ted hadn't been waiting an hour. Twinkle pushed through the last stand of corn and came out into the open place beside the rock.

"What took you so long?" demanded Ted, glaring at Sue. Every time Ted looked at Sue he

knew he was seeing himself. The twins both had brown hair, blue eyes, and round faces sprinkled with freckles.

"What's your idea now?" asked Sue, who knew she had come as fast as she could.

Instead of answering, Ted jabbed an elbow into Sue's side. He pointed to a wooden sledge near the rock. It had two straps hitched at one end.

"What's that for?" asked Sue, rubbing her side.

"A rock drag," said Ted proudly. "I made it out of that old window shutter in the shed. Mother said Daddy wouldn't care."

Sue hated to admit she didn't see the use of a rock drag. She waited for Ted to explain.

"Get it?" asked Ted. "Twinkle's going to pull it and we're going to clean the rocks out of that place in the brook and make a dam for a swimming pool."

His voice was loud with pride. The idea of a swimming pool was one of the best he had ever had.

Sue looked toward the brook which ran

through the meadow below the rock. It was a quiet stream, winding a narrow course through the meadow grass. Daisies and clover nodded their heads over the water. Small dark fish lay in the shadow of the high banks.

"Don't you see?" demanded Ted. "Right where the brook turns there's a shallow pool. If we make a dam it'll be deep enough to swim in."

"We can't swim," said Sue. "We never had any place to learn."

"Now's our chance," said Ted. "Come on."

He tied the sledge to Twinkle's saddle and urged him on. "This stupid saddle's no good for this work. I wish we had a western saddle. This pad's baby stuff."

"It's better for Robby," said Sue. "Pete says it's a beginner's saddle."

"Well, we're no beginners and this isn't Robby's pony. You just give him rides to keep him quiet."

"I'm teaching him to ride," said Sue, skipping to keep up with Ted. "He can hold the reins and everything now."

"And quack at him," said Ted. "Robby thinks everything's a duck. Lucky Jemima can understand him."

Sue laughed. "Jemima's cross as two sticks. She's been sitting in Twinkle's manger for two days, pecking at everybody."

"Never mind Jemima," said Ted. "Here we are. Look!"

They had reached the bend in the stream and Ted pointed. Just beyond the pool the brook narrowed and plunged into a rocky ravine.

"We can get rocks from the ravine and pile them at the narrow place," said Ted. "We'll have a real pool, maybe four feet deep."

Ted's idea began to seem real to Sue. The water looked cool and inviting. Sun specks danced on the pool's surface. She looked at Ted and nodded. "Let's go," she said.

It was hot, hard work but Ted and Sue kept at it. They wrested stones from the ravine, heaped them on the sledge, and made Twinkle haul them to the dam. They put the largest stones at the bottom and calked them with mud and grass. Medium-sized stones went on top.

Before long Ted and Sue were dripping with mud and water. They had taken off their shoes and stockings and rolled up their jeans. But they were wet from head to foot.

"What are we going to put on top of the dam?" asked Sue at last. "These little stones will wash away."

Ted looked around. "Those two stones," he said, pointing to two flat rocks on the bank. "Hey, the water's deeper already!"

Sue saw that Ted was right. The dam was holding the water in the pool. The surface was darker and quieter.

"It's almost done!" cried Sue. "Hurry up with those stones."

Ted grabbed the edge of one of the stones and pulled mightily. His face got red and his breath grew short. He couldn't budge the stone. Sue helped. Her face grew redder than Ted's. They tied Twinkle's straps to the stone and made him pull. Nothing helped.

Ted and Sue were ready to give up when a voice said, "Why don't you pick on something your own size, Ted?"

"Pete!" shouted Ted and Sue both at once.

"Wobby here, too," said Robby from his perch on Pete's shoulder.

Ted and Sue explained about the pool and the dam in loud, excited voices. They both talked at once. But Pete understood. You never had to tell Pete things twice.

"Well now, let's see," said Pete. He put Robby on the ground and bent over the big stone. His arms were brown and lean, and his muscles were strong. His big hands closed over the edge of the stone.

"Wobby help," said Robby. He planted his blanket on the ground and sat down heavily on the stone.

"Thanks," said Pete. He lifted Robby in the air. Just as Robby opened his mouth to roar, Pete sat him on Twinkle's back. Sue was ready with the blanket. She stuffed it into Robby's arms. Robby was happy. He had a fine view of everything.

"Now," said Pete. He bent over the stone once more. But suddenly he stood up and looked at Ted and Sue. "Either of you seen my cowbell? The round silver one your dad got in New York?"

The twins shook their heads blankly. Pete bent down again. "Sure is funny," he said. "This morning it was hanging on the doorpost in the barn. Now it's took itself off. I set real store by that bell. Didn't even see fit to let one of the cows wear it."

But Ted and Sue weren't interested in the cowbell. They were too busy admiring the way Pete handled the big stone. He lifted it from the ground to the dam as easily as though he were carrying a sack of meal. In five minutes both stones were on top of the dam. Ted and Sue packed them with mud and grass. The dam was finished.

They stood back to look at it. The water in the pool was still and brown. You couldn't even see the gravel on the bottom.

"Let's go swimming!" said Ted.

"Fim, fim!" shouted Robby, waving his blanket. "Wobby fim."

"Wobby drown more'n likely," said Pete. "Look here, you two, you ain't ducks. You gotta learn to swim. Start with the dead-man's float."

"What's that?" said Ted and Sue in one breath.

"You lay out on the water, holdin' your breath," said Pete. "You dassn't move so much as a finger. The dead-man's float, see?"

The twins nodded, but they looked doubtful.

"Best way to start learnin' to swim," said Pete. "Tell you what. The first one learns to float the longest gets a prize. Anything in this world you want is the prize."

2 *Dead-Man's Float*

"HEY, quit kicking me!"

Ted rose sputtering to the surface of the new swimming pool and glared at Sue's back. She was stretched full length on the water, her brown hair floating like a web around her head. Ted watched her carefully and saw her feet wriggle.

"No fair!" he shouted. "Pete says you can't move. You've got to float like a dead man." He poked Sue to make sure she heard.

Sue stood up gasping. Her face was bright red, her hair hung to her shoulders in wet strings.

"Stop punching me," she said angrily. "How can I win if you bother me when I'm practicing?"

"Who says you're going to win?" asked Ted. He sat down on the bank, his forehead wrinkled with thought. "I'm going to ask for a western saddle for a prize," he said suddenly.

Twinkle, who was eating grass near the bank, whinnied at the sound of his voice. Robby was perched on Twinkle's back watching the twins. "Taddle," said Robby. "Wobby wanta taddle."

Sue laughed. "If you two want a 'taddle' you might both get a surprise. Suppose I win?"

Ted stared at her. Sue really seemed to think she might win. A small nagging doubt crept into his mind. Suppose Sue *did* win? In the week they had been practicing the dead-man's float Sue had learned to hold her breath almost as long as he could.

"Well," said Ted loudly, "if you do win, you'll ask for a western saddle. Anyone with brains knows we need it more than anything."

Sue didn't answer. She hated to tell Ted she couldn't decide what she wanted if she won. A saddle seemed rather a tame prize when Pete had said you could have anything in the world.

"Mother and Daddy are going to be judges," she said finally.

But Ted wasn't going to let Sue change the subject. "You *are* going to ask for a western saddle, aren't you?"

Sue shrugged her shoulders. "Maybe," she said. Then she took a deep breath and threw herself down on the water.

Ted watched her with a worried frown. She really could do the dead-man's float for a long time. She wasn't wriggling her toes now either. Girls, he thought desperately. You never could tell about them. Didn't she know a western saddle was the most important thing in the world?

He was too upset to practice any more that afternoon. The top of the big rock was his dressing room and in two minutes he had changed to his jeans and shirt.

"I'll take Twinkle," he shouted.

"I promised Robby a ride home," cried Sue from the pool.

"Rats!" said Ted. It was no use arguing with Sue when she had promised Robby something.

He jumped off the rock and climbed up through the cornfield to the house. Up in his room he pulled his treasure box from beneath his bed. The box was a wooden chest painted red. In it he kept all the things he valued most. Sue had a treasure box, too. Hers was painted blue.

Ted began arranging his lead soldiers, his coins, and the stones he kept in the box. The stones were his favorite things. He had pieces of quartz, mica, agate, and crystal that he had collected around the farm. His best stone was a white quartz, round, smooth, and polished.

"Hey!" Ted shouted without realizing it. He

leaned down to look again. He counted all the stones. He was right. The white quartz was missing.

"Who took my stone?" Ted was yelling now.

No one heard him. He jumbled the things back in the box and ran downstairs. When he reached the yard Sue was just coming up from the corn-field leading Twinkle. Robby was in the saddle, the reins in both hands. Pete was watching from the barn door.

"You'll make a jockey of him yet, Sue girl," said Pete. "Good ridin', Robby. Hang on with—"

But Pete never finished his sentence. Ted cut him off short with a great shout of rage. "Who took my piece of quartz? Where is it, Sue? Hand it over."

Sue stared at Ted. She knew how Ted valued the white stone. Now he was accusing her of taking it. She was angry, hurt, and sorry all at once. Tears came into her eyes.

"Where is it?" demanded Ted again.

"Ted," said Pete. His voice was quiet and firm. When he spoke like that you had to listen. Ted knew what he meant, too.

He looked at Sue's face. "Okay, Sue," he muttered. "But I'd like to know who took it."

"I'd like to know where my cowbell is," said Pete. "Maybe I mislaid it. Maybe you mislaid your quartz piece. It sure is a puzzle."

"You ought to be more careful of things," said Sue. She spoke sharply for she was still angry.

Robby took his thumb out of his mouth and pointed at the chickens scratching in the barnyard. "Yeggs," he said. "Chickies' yeggs."

Pete laughed. "Robby's got the right idea. Let's change the subject. Who's goin' to win the dead-man's float?"

"Whoever wins is going to ask for a western saddle for a prize," said Ted. He looked straight at Sue, but she tossed her head at him.

Pete gulped. He looked a little worried. "How about you, Sue?"

"I haven't decided," said Sue. But if she won, she had made up her mind not to ask for a western saddle. Ted couldn't accuse her of taking his old piece of quartz and expect her to ask for a saddle.

"Better put your mind on it," said Pete. "Contest's tomorrow. Tell you what. I'm takin' the horses to the village for feed. You two come along. Maybe you'll see something in the store you want, Sue."

Ted and Sue were delighted at the idea. Riding behind Chub and Nellie in the box wagon was one of their favorite treats. They didn't often get a chance to go to the village. There were two stores there and a railroad station. If they were in luck they might see the New York train go by.

"I'll ask Mother," said Sue, her anger forgotten. "Come on, Robby, I'll take you into the house."

But Robby had other plans. He had heard the word "wagon" and he knew what it meant. Before Sue could catch him, he slid from the saddle and ran toward the barn.

The wagon was in the doorway. He clambered over the wheel and settled himself in the back. Then he looked over the wagon's side at Sue. His thumb was in his mouth, his blanket under one arm. He was ready to go.

"Kinda knows his own mind, Sue," said Pete. "Let him come. You hurry along and get ready."

Mother nodded and smiled when Sue asked if they could go. She knew how the twins loved to ride in the wagon. Sue ran upstairs to put on a clean jersey. As she pulled it over her head she saw her blue treasure box under her bed.

It wouldn't take a minute to see if all her things were safe. She dragged out the box and hastily counted over her treasures. The shells, the illustrated copy of *Little Women*, and the dolls' tea set were all there. Even her glass doorknob was in its corner.

The doorknob was her best treasure. She had found it in the attic. It was cut and polished so it looked like a huge diamond. Sue hoped it was. It might be glass but you couldn't be sure it wasn't a diamond.

Sue tucked it into the pocket of her jeans. Pete and Ted had lost things, and she didn't want to lose her diamond doorknob. It made a big lump in her pocket as she ran out to get into the wagon.

"My turn to ride on the seat with Pete," said Ted, as soon as Sue appeared.

Pete nodded. "That's right. I been keeping track. Hop in with Robby, Sue."

Sue didn't argue. If Pete said it was Ted's turn, she knew it must be. Pete was never wrong and he was always fair.

She put one arm around Robby's shoulders to steady him from the jolting of the wagon. The two black horses moved forward. They were on their way to the village. It was over a mile away and they had a long time to enjoy the ride. No one said much. It was more fun to watch the branches of the trees lacing overhead and listen to the firm clopping of the horses' hoofs on the road.

By the time they reached the village Robby

was asleep. He lay with his head pillowed on his blanket curled into one corner of the wagon.

"Leave him," said Pete. "He's got too many fingers for a store. There's nothin' he don't want to see with them fingers either."

Pete went to get the bags of grain and load them in the wagon. He let Ted and Sue go to the hardware store by themselves. The store sold everything from dish mops to lawn mowers. You could spend hours in such a wonderful place.

Sue hadn't been in the store five minutes before she saw just what she wanted. It was a box of paints in little bottles. There were twelve bright colors and two brushes.

"There," said Sue, "that's it."

Ted grunted. "Who wants paints?"

"I do," said Sue decidedly. "Look, the colors are made of powder. You have to mix them with water. It says so." She pointed to the directions on the box.

Ted started to say what he thought of the paints, then he decided not to. He knew Sue had made up her mind. The only way to get the western saddle was to win the dead-man's float himself.

On the way home Pete made Robby sit in front with him. Ted and Sue sat on the pile of feed bags. It was a high, wobbly perch and the twins pretended they were on a camel's back.

"I'm going to ask for a box of paints if I win," Sue told Pete when they were almost home.

"That's more like it," said Pete. "I kinda hope you—" But Pete didn't say any more. He never

took sides, not even between a western saddle and a box of paints.

The next morning Mother and Daddy came to the swimming pool to judge the contest. They looked very solemn because this was an important event. Pete came too, carrying Robby. Robby's blanket was tied around his waist for safekeeping. He knew something exciting was about to happen and he kicked his heels for joy.

"Take it easy, old feller," said Pete. "I'm no football."

Robby saw Ted and Sue waiting by the pool and gave a bounce. "Down, down," he commanded, kicking Pete once more to show he meant it.

"Happy to oblige," said Pete, putting Robby
on the ground.

Robby ran to Sue and threw his arms around
her knees. For once Sue paid no attention to him.
She felt as though a butter churn were turning
inside her. Her hands and feet were cold. She
shivered. She tried to think of the paints, but the
colors danced crazily before her eyes.

"What's the matter?" asked Ted, his teeth
chattering. "It's not cold. You don't have to
shiver." His voice shook. In a few moments he

would know whether he had won the western saddle or not.

"All set?" asked Pete. He sounded as though nothing special were happening. But his eyes were brighter than usual.

"A-all s-set," said the twins together.

Daddy got out his watch with the second hand. Mother held Robby's hand.

"On your mark," said Pete, "get set—"

A horrible pause followed. Ted and Sue waited for the magic word.

"GO!" shouted Pete.

"Do," shrieked Robby. He yanked away from Mother and plunged into the water at the twins' heels. A fearful splashing followed. Arms and

legs and heads churned the water into a fury of waves. Ted and Sue came up sputtering. Robby floundered helplessly in the water.

"Get him out!" shouted Mother.

Daddy and Pete lifted the sodden Robby from the pool. He was choking, his face was scarlet. "Wobby fim," he gasped.

Ted and Sue only glared at Robby. Pete took him firmly under one arm. Once again he gave the starting signal. Once again Ted and Sue dove into the pool. They held their breath and floated.

3 *The Artistic-Detective Club*

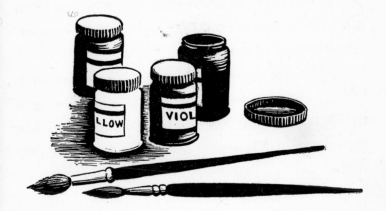

THERE was water in Sue's nose and in her ears. Something heavy pressed on her chest. In another minute she would have to stand up. If only she knew what Ted was doing. She thought about the paintbox. The row of little bottles was like a rainbow in her mind.

"Hang on," she told herself, "hang on, hang on."

Ted lay perfectly still on the water. It seemed to pull him down. For a second he wondered if he was drowning. Then he remembered the water was only four feet deep. He concentrated fiercely on the western saddle. Maybe Pete would get one with silver embossed on it.

"You've got to win," he said inside himself.

His last breath was gone. If he swallowed some water maybe it would be the same as a breath of air. He opened his mouth and gulped.

Suddenly it was just as though a firecracker had exploded inside him. Ted had to stand up. He floundered to his feet, choking on that mouthful of water. Then he shook his head hard and looked down.

There at his feet was Sue. She was still floating, her arms stretched over her head. Ted knew Sue had won the dead-man's float. For one horrible second he wanted to cry. Then he remembered he couldn't. Instead he leaned down and touched Sue's shoulder.

"You won!" he bellowed. "You won, Sue!"

Sue heard and struggled to her feet. She couldn't speak. She just looked at Ted, wondering if it was really true that she had won. Then came a great shout from the bank.

"Good girl, Sue," cried Mother and Daddy both together.

"Nice goin', Sue girl," said Pete in his quietest voice.

"Too, Too," shouted Robby. He was held tightly under Pete's arm, but he waved his blanket like a flag.

Sue tried not to look too pleased. She almost wished Ted had won, because he wanted the saddle so much. She looked at him with a funny embarrassed feeling.

Ted nodded at her, his lips held in a firm line. "Nice work," he said.

A balloon of happiness swelled inside Sue. Those two words from Ted were better than anything the others had said. Now she really felt she had won.

"You can use the paints too," she told Ted, as they waded from the pool.

"Okay," said Ted. He watched the others patting Sue on the back. He knew now what a great mistake he had made in swallowing that mouthful of water. If he hadn't he might have won. He started to tell about it. Then he saw Sue's face.

It was flushed with joy, her eyes were like candles. Ted shut his mouth tightly.

"You know," said Pete, as they all walked up through the cornfield together, "I'm kinda relieved Sue won. Western saddles come high."

Ted felt comforted. Maybe Pete wouldn't have given him a saddle if he had won. "When are you going to get the paintbox?" he asked.

"Soon's the law allows," was all Pete would promise.

The paintbox came that afternoon. Pete made a special trip to the village to get it. He put it into Sue's hands as though he were handing her a crown of diamonds.

"Thanks, Pete," said Sue. She couldn't tell him how she felt. You never can find the right words when you are especially grateful.

Pete always knew how you felt. "That's all right," he said. His voice was quite gruff.

Sue looked at the rows of colors. "I'm going to put it right in my treasure box," she said.

"Aren't you going to use it?" cried Ted. "What's the point of—"

But Sue wasn't listening. She was already run-

ning toward her room with the paints held tight in both hands.

"Good *night!*" shouted Ted. Then in a flash an idea came to him. He had thought of a way to make use of the paintbox. He raced for the stone wall to write a message to Sue.

Up in her room Sue pulled her treasure box from under her bed. As she fitted the paintbox into one corner, she knew something was wrong. The treasure box didn't look the way it usually did. Something was missing. Sue scrabbled hurriedly through her treasures, hoping she had made a mistake.

"Where's my diamond doorknob?" Her voice was a long wail. Then she remembered taking it to the village. It must have dropped from her pocket in the wagon.

Sue was downstairs and in the barnyard in two seconds. She heard Ted signaling from the shed.

"Eeeee-ow! Eeeee-ow!"

Sue didn't bother to answer, but dove into the back of the wagon. There were bits of hay and a scattering of oats on the floor of the wagon, but no diamond doorknob. She looked all over the barn and in the yard. The diamond doorknob had disappeared.

"It's gone!" cried Sue. "I lost it!"

Pete was in the grain room and heard her. "Now what?" he asked.

Sue explained in a tearful voice. Ted, who had grown tired of waiting in the shed, came into the barn and heard her.

"There's a robber around here," he announced. "We better watch out."

Pete scratched his head. "I'll ask at the hardware store," he said. "Maybe you dropped it
there." Pete took a hoe and went off to the potato
lot. He had spoken calmly, but Sue knew he was
bothered by the way things were disappearing
from the farm.

She sighed heavily. The diamond doorknob
meant even more to her than the new paintbox.

"Hey," said Ted, "snap out of it! Didn't you
hear my signal?"

Sue nodded unhappily.

"Well, get busy and— Hey, make a getaway!"
Ted disappeared in the direction of the shed.

Sue saw Robby trotting across the yard. He was headed straight for her and he looked as though he had important business at hand.

For a second Sue didn't know which way to go. If she hid in Twinkle's stall, Robby would be sure to find her. He often went to give Twinkle a pat when he came into the barn.

Then she heard Robby's welcoming cry. "Too, Too!"

Without thinking she made a dash for the stairs leading to the grain room. She hated to

run away from Robby. But it was one of Ted's firmest rules that she must visit the stone wall hiding place alone.

She heard Robby's feet pattering on the floor below. He was coming toward the stairs. Sue looked hurriedly around her. The hay chutes that led down to the mangers were right beside her. The one nearest the wall went down to Twinkle's manger. She slid over the edge of the hole, held on for a second, then dropped.

It wasn't a long fall. She landed right beside Jemima, who was in her favorite place near Twinkle. Jemima objected to sudden visitors, especially ones who dropped on her from above. She pecked sharply at Sue's back.

"Ouch!" cried Sue, jumping from the manger in a hurry.

Twinkle wasn't surprised to see Sue coming from his manger. He knew enough to expect anything from the twins. He just stepped politely to one side to let Sue pass him.

"Good old Twinkle," whispered Sue and gave him a quick pat.

She listened and heard Robby greet the setting hen in the grain room. He was safely out of the way and Sue ran toward the stone wall.

"Meet me in the workroom. Important. Get rid of Robby," was the message Sue found on the pad.

She had taken care of the last part of Ted's order. Now to find out his new idea. The workroom was over the shed and she knew he was waiting for her there.

"What kept you so long?" demanded Ted, when Sue's head appeared at the top of the ladder which led to the workroom.

"What's important now?" asked Sue by way of answer.

Ted forgot his impatience. His eyes sparkled as he explained his latest plan. "We'll have a club. A painting club. Now you've got those paints they might as well be useful."

Sue started to say the paints were hers. But she knew that sooner or later Ted would find a way to use them. "What'll we paint?" she asked instead.

Ted frowned. Sometimes girls had no imagination. "Things," he said grandly. Then he lowered his voice mysteriously. "This club will be a detective club, too. We've got to find out who's taking stuff around here."

"I don't see how we can paint and do detective work at the same time," said Sue. "What'll we call the club?"

This was something Ted hadn't thought about. He knew Sue didn't think much of his new idea. He would have to get a good name for the club to make her see the advantages of it. He thought busily. Then the name came to him.

"It's called the Artistic-Detective Club," he announced. "The ADC for short and anyone who tells what the initials mean is banished from the club forever."

"Okay," said Sue.

Ted felt better. "You get the paints and a couple of tin cans for water," he said. "Keep away from Robby. He'd ruin all those paints."

Sue had no difficulty avoiding Robby. He was nowhere to be seen as she crossed the yard to the house. She noticed that Twinkle was in the barnyard standing beneath the elm tree with Chub and Nellie. Pete must have come back and let Twinkle out. Probably Robby was with Pete.

Sue sighed as she opened her treasure box. She hated to see the empty corner where she had kept her diamond doorknob. Ted's idea of doing detective work was a good one after all. Anything they could do to find the diamond doorknob suited Sue.

"What do detectives do?" she asked when she returned to the workroom with the tin cans and paintbox.

Ted was busy piling wooden blocks on the workbench and didn't answer right away. "Two for you, two for me," he muttered, dividing the blocks into separate heaps. Then he noticed Sue. "Detectives detect things naturally. Find clues, follow trails, and listen to things. You detect first and I'll paint. I'm going to make a picture on one of these blocks."

Sue backed away, clutching her paints. "Whose paints are they, anyway?" she demanded. "If you know so much about detecting, you do it first."

Ted hesitated, but only for a minute. "We'll both paint," he said.

Once the dry paints were mixed with water the twins set to work. Soon they had covered several blocks with bright smears of paint. The pictures were wet and sticky and it was hard to

tell what they were meant to be. But the twins felt very artistic.

At last they heard Mother calling. "Robby! Robby, where are you?"

"Time for supper," said Sue. "Let's go."

"Where's Robby?" asked Mother the minute she saw Ted and Sue. "Pete says he hasn't seen him since early afternoon."

Sue remembered her escape from Robby. She also remembered that she hadn't seen him since. "Maybe he's in the barn," she said hopefully.

"Pete's looked everywhere," said Mother. "We've hunted and hunted."

Sue's heart gave a painful thud. If she hadn't run away from Robby he wouldn't be lost now.

"Now's the time for some real detective work," said Ted.

"Don't try to be funny," said Sue fiercely. "Let's hunt for him."

In the barn they found Daddy and Pete talking together in low, worried voices. Pete had looked all over the barn and Daddy had been everywhere on the farm. Robby was nowhere to be found.

It was getting late. Long evening shadows stretched across the barnyard. Soon the sun would go down. They called and hunted. But there was no answering cry from Robby.

4 *Detective Jemima*

I'VE called all the neighbors," said Mother. "They haven't seen him."

She came out to join the others in the barn. Sue knew she couldn't bear to stay in the house and do nothing about finding Robby.

It was hard not to cry. Sue wanted to, but Mother wasn't crying. She only looked quiet and her eyes watched Daddy.

They stood in a circle on the barn floor. No one said anything. The western sky beyond the barnyard was streaked with bright clouds. The sun was like a huge red ball hanging on the far hills.

"Might as well light the lantern," said Pete. His voice was queer and heavy. It made the twins feel worse just to hear his solemn words.

The lantern made a round glow of light on the dusty floor. Suddenly Pete stamped his foot. "He's gotta be somewhere," he said in a loud voice.

"Quack," said Jemima from Twinkle's stall. She sounded cross. No one paid any attention to her. "Quack, quack, quack." Jemima flopped out of the manger and waddled from the stall.

She looked at the circle of people waiting in the lantern light. She seemed angrier than ever. "Quack," she said fiercely. Then she lifted her head in the air and paddled past them to the barnyard.

Ted watched Jemima. It was better to look at her than stand there doing nothing. In the gray light he saw Jemima go straight to Twinkle who still stood under the elm tree.

Twinkle lowered his head to welcome Jemima. He whinnied softly and Jemima quacked in a loud scolding voice. It was easy to see that Jemima was complaining about something.

"Look at those two," said Ted. "What's ailing Jemima?"

But no one was interested in Jemima or Twinkle now. Everyone was too busy trying to think of another place to look for Robby.

Then Ted saw Jemima turn away from Twinkle and start for the barn. She looked back at Twinkle and quacked. Twinkle whinnied again in a questioning way.

A perfect fury of quacks burst from Jemima. It sounded as though she was telling Twinkle just what she thought of him.

"That duck's sure givin' Twinkle what-for," said Pete.

When Pete spoke everyone looked at Jemima. You couldn't help but notice her now. Once more she began to waddle toward the barn. This time Twinkle followed her. Jemima saw that Twinkle was obeying her and quacked in a way that meant, "It's about time."

Jemima marched straight to Twinkle's stall and hopped up into the manger. Twinkle was right behind her.

"Quack, quack," said Jemima.

Twinkle neighed. He sounded startled.

"Something's up," said Pete. He started for the stall, carrying the lantern.

But Ted got ahead of him. Even before Pete spoke a strange and wonderful thought had come to him. He ducked under Pete's arm and reached the manger first.

It was too dark to see anything, but Ted stretched out his hand. His fingers felt something soft. He reached further. He touched a snub nose and a round, warm cheek.

"*Robby!*" yelled Ted.

Pete lifted the lantern high. Its rays fell down on Robby, curled tightly into a corner of the manger. His thumb was in his mouth, his blanket rolled into a ball under his head.

Mother, Daddy, and Sue crowded into the stall. Twinkle was jammed against the wall, but he didn't mind. He just whinnied once or twice to remind people he was still there.

Daddy lifted the sleeping Robby from the manger. Mother grabbed him and hugged him. Tears streamed down Sue's face.

Ted looked at Pete. Pete swallowed so hard his head jerked. Then Ted didn't mind if his eyes felt blurry.

Robby opened his eyes. He smiled a large, pleased smile. "Wobby feep," he remarked.

Pete rubbed his head. "And I thought I'd looked into every knothole in this barn," he said. "How'd he get here? He could reach in here with his hands, but it's too high for his kind of climbin'."

Sue remembered her escape from Robby. He must have guessed she had gone down the chute and followed her. She felt it was all her fault. But

she told what had happened. Her voice shook as she spoke.

" 'Twasn't your fault," said Pete, who knew how she felt. "Fixin' to take a nap in a horse manger is just one of Robby's bright ideas. It would take a detective to know what he's goin' to do next."

" 'Tective," said Robby sleepily.

"Jemima's the detective," said Ted. "She told Twinkle Robby was in the manger. I know she did." He reached into the manger to give Jemima a pat of congratulation.

But Jemima didn't care for praise. She pecked at Ted's hand.

"Twinkle was smart too," said Sue. "He knew enough to follow Jemima."

Twinkle didn't mind at all when Sue hugged him.

Robby was carefully inspected for bumps and bruises, but none were found. The hay in the manger had softened his fall. He was carried from the barn on Daddy's shoulders.

" 'By yeggs," said Robby as they crossed the yard.

"What'll he say next?" asked Ted. He tried to sound disgusted. But you couldn't be cross with Robby when he had been lost and was found again.

After breakfast the next morning Ted ran to the barn. It was his job to help Pete feed and water the horses while Sue helped Mother make the beds. Robby trotted after Ted and went straight to Twinkle's stall.

"Find another roost," said Ted, when Robby

settled himself on the straw under Twinkle's nose. "You're in the way and I'm in a hurry."

He couldn't wait to get to the workroom. A new idea for the Artistic-Detective Club had just come to him. He had told Sue to meet him there in fifteen minutes.

"Move, can't you, Robby?" he demanded.

Robby took his thumb out of his mouth. "No," he said and put his thumb back where he liked it.

Ted dumped an armful of hay into the manger and was rewarded with another peck from Jemima's hard bill. "What's got into everybody?" asked Ted, rubbing his hand.

"It's you that's got the hump," said Pete from Chub's stall. "Ever hear that haste makes waste?"

Ted growled under his breath. "Someone's got to watch Robby," he said. "Sue and I have work to do and we can't have Robby messing around."

"Who says he wants to come with you? Robby and I are goin' up to the ten-acre lot to do a little hayin'."

Ted felt ashamed of himself. He knew he and Sue ought to share the responsibility of looking after Robby. After last night's trouble Daddy had said that someone must be with him all the time.

"We'll watch him this afternoon," he said hurriedly and ran for the shed.

"Don't overwork that brain of yours," Pete called after him.

Ted didn't answer. Pete was always teasing. He found that Sue had reached the clubroom before him and was painting a flowerpot with sprays of goldenrod. The blossoms were very yellow and the leaves very green.

"Mother said I could have the pots," she said before Ted could object.

"Never mind the pots," said Ted. "Listen, I've thought of something. You know how people always put up notices if they lose things. We're going to paint a sign and list all the things we've lost around here."

Sue painted another goldenrod blossom. She didn't say anything.

Ted kicked at the leg of the workbench. "Don't you see how it will mean we're doing both artistic and detective work at the same time? What's the matter with you?"

"Where'll we put the sign when it's finished?" asked Sue.

Ted hadn't thought of that. He frowned and searched his brain hurriedly for an idea. "In the post office in the village," he announced after a minute. "There are lots of signs there."

Sue put down her paintbrush. She nodded at Ted. Instantly he felt better. He chose a square board from their supply of painting materials.

"You make a list of the things we've lost," said Ted. "I'll paint in the background." He smeared red paint over the board in a wet mass.

Sue sighed. She wasn't surprised to find that Ted was going to do the painting while she wrote a list. "Let's see," she said, licking a pencil. "Pete's cowbell, your piece of quartz, and *my* diamond doorknob." She sighed again as she thought of the shining doorknob.

"Funny," said Ted in an absent-minded way, "they are all round things." He looked at the smeared paint. "This is going to take a year to dry. We can't paint on the list until it does."

He glanced out the window toward the distant cornfield. Beyond the waving green blades he saw the glimmering water of the swimming pool. It was stuffy in the workroom. A swim would be wonderful.

"Guess I'll take a look around while this dries," said Ted. The next minute he was hanging by his hands from the window ledge. He dropped to the ground with a thud. Once out of Sue's sight he began to run.

Left alone Sue wiped the smeared paint from

the board and rubbed it dry with a cloth. Now the background was a nice, even pink color. She began to paint the list of lost articles. When she finished the sign said:

LOST STRAYED OR STOLEN

1 round silver cowbell, Pete's.

1 piece of quartz, white, Ted's.

1 Doorknob, maybe diamond, Sue's.

The letters were rather uneven, but they were done in a shiny black and showed plainly on the pink board. Sue painted a border of blue and yellow flowers and the sign was done.

When she took it into the house at lunch time everyone admired it. Even Ted nodded approvingly.

"Not bad," he said. "Let's take it to the post office this afternoon. Your turn to harness Twinkle."

Sue never minded harnessing Twinkle. It was fun to fit on the collar, attach the traces to the whiffletree, and strap on the bridle.

Twinkle always stood very still when he was being harnessed. He loved to go driving with the cart.

Robby had followed Sue to the barn. Before she was ready to back Twinkle between the shafts Robby was firmly planted on one of the red seats of the cart. He wanted to make sure he wasn't left behind. His blanket was stuffed safely behind the leather flap under the seat.

"Do we have to take Robby?" asked Ted, when he came into the barn.

Pete, who was standing nearby ready to help Sue if she needed it, cleared his throat with a loud noise. Then Ted remembered he had promised to look after Robby that afternoon.

"Okay," said Ted quickly.

Sue was ready at last. It was the rule that whoever did the harnessing got first turn to drive. She picked up the reins and slapped them gently on Twinkle's back.

"Giddy yap," she said.

"Wap, wap," cried Robby and bounced on the seat.

Twinkle didn't move. He looked toward his stall and neighed softly.

"Haven't you forgotten something?" asked Pete.

"Jemima!" cried Ted and Sue together.

But when Pete went to get Jemima from Twinkle's manger she didn't want to come. She quacked furiously, but Pete was firm with her. He knew Twinkle wouldn't go without Jemima. He carried the protesting Jemima from the stall and plumped her down beside Robby.

"What's the matter with her lately?" asked Sue. "She never used to be so cross."

"Settin'," said Pete. "She's got a lot on her mind these days. Get along now." He slapped Twinkle's flank and the cart moved forward.

Jemima flapped her wings and tried to get out of the cart. Ted made a grab for her and caught her by one foot. Jemima squawked and Robby shouted.

Twinkle began to trot. He whirled down the drive and turned into the road at a brisk clip. Jemima struggled to get free. Ted hung onto her with both hands. The noise and confusion was at its height when Twinkle began to gallop.

"D-do s-something about t-that d-duck," cried Sue, her voice jolting with every motion of the cart. She pulled on the reins with all her might.

Then Robby reached out and put both arms around Jemima. Instantly Jemima stopped quacking. She sat down on Robby's lap and rested her head on his arm. Twinkle slowed from a gallop to a trot, then to a walk. All was peaceful in the cart once more.

"It's lucky Jemima likes Robby," said Sue.

"Quack," said Robby, patting Jemima.

"Quack," said Jemima comfortably.

"Some duck," said Ted.

The postmaster scratched his head when he saw the sign. "Guess there's no law saying you can't hang that sign," he said at last. "Here's a nail and hammer. Go to it."

Ted hung the sign right by the door where everyone could see it. Sue stood back to admire her handiwork. There were several other notices and signs on the wall but none showed up as hers did. She nodded approvingly at it.

"Say!" Ted's exclamation made Sue jump. She saw he was pointing to another sign right beside hers. She began to read it hastily.

COUNTY FAIR
Come One, Come All

Before she could finish Ted pointed to a line of type at the bottom of the sign. Sue bent forward to read it.

"Exhibition of Pony Riding," she read aloud. "Prizes Given."

The twins looked at each other. The same

thought was in both their minds in one moment.

"The fair's one week from today," said Ted in a low voice.

Sue nodded.

"Prizes," said Ted.

Again Sue nodded.

There was a short pause. Then Ted said it first. "I claim to ride Twinkle at the fair!"

"No," said Sue, "I'm going to."

"No, me," cried Ted.

"Me, me, me!" shouted Robby, who didn't like to be left out of things.

5 Blue Paint

THE argument lasted all the way home. They kept it up while they unharnessed Twinkle and put him in his stall. They talked about it while they watered and fed him.

"I said I claimed to ride him first," said Ted. It was a remark he had made many times.

"I don't care," said Sue. "Twinkle's my pony too." She had said this before, but it made no impression on Ted.

Pete was tossing hay down the chutes and whistling softly. He sounded as though he was trying to drown out the noise of the dispute.

Robby was perched on an overturned bucket in Twinkle's stall. He didn't bother to listen to Ted and Sue. He was having a private conversation with Jemima, who peered down at him from the manger.

"I'm going to ride him and that's the end of it!" shouted Ted.

"I am," said Sue.

Pete's voice came hollowly down the hay chute. "Seems to me you're gettin' nowhere fast."

"Sue's just stubborn," said Ted.

"Ted is," said Sue.

"That makes it mutual," said Pete. He clumped down the grain-room stairs and came into Twinkle's stall. Ted and Sue looked up at Pete. They both knew he would think of some way to settle the argument.

Pete leaned against the side of the stall and chewed a straw. "To begin with," he said, "suppose you tell me what the fight's all about."

The twins both began to talk at once and very fast. But Pete was used to listening to them and understood everything. He nodded solemnly when they finished. Then he took the straw from his mouth and broke it into two pieces, one long and one short. He held the bits of straw hidden in his hands.

"Draw lots," he said.

Ted and Sue looked at each other. It was the only fair thing to do and it was just like Pete to have thought of it.

"Okay?" asked Ted.

Sue nodded slowly, "Okay, but—"

"But what?" demanded Ted.

"I don't want to do it now," said Sue in a burst. "Let's wait until the last minute."

Nothing Pete or Ted could say made Sue change her mind. She couldn't bear to know who was to have the honor of riding Twinkle at the fair. Suppose she lost the draw? She would have nothing to look forward to.

"Maybe Sue's right," said Pete at last. "You'll both have to practice on Twinkle and it'll do you a power of good."

"We'll start now," cried Ted. "I claim first turn to—"

But Pete interrupted him. "Not today you don't," he said. "Twinkle's been trottin' enough for one day. It won't do to wear him out before the big day."

Ted knew there was no further use in arguing. "Guess I'll go up to the clubroom," he said. "Come on, Sue."

But Sue shook her head. "I've got something else to do," she said.

"What?" demanded Ted.

But Sue just looked mysterious. She had a book and two apples in her hayloft hideaway. But Ted didn't have to know everything she did.

Ted departed for the clubroom, muttering something about "girls" under his breath. He saw Robby start after him, trailing his blanket. Ted began to run.

"Way, Wobby," cried Robby, beginning to trot.

"Find Sue," shouted Ted and disappeared up the ladder to the clubroom.

An outburst of wails followed after him, but gradually the sound faded away and Ted forgot about Robby. He began to paint a "No Trespassing" sign, using blue paint. Maybe if he hung it at the end of the drive, it would keep anyone away who came to steal something else from the farm.

He was just putting the finishing touches to the sign when he heard Pete calling the cows in the lane. Ted jumped to his feet. There was something he had to ask Pete right away. For a second he looked at the blue paint bottle. It was his own rule that the paints had to be put away in the box after they were used.

"Ho, boss! Co, boss!" shouted Pete.

Ted forgot the paints. He scrambled out through the window and ran toward the cow barn.

"Where's Sue?" asked Pete. "Robby with her?"

"I told him to find her," said Ted. "Hey, Pete, what do you think the prize will be at the fair?"

"I'm givin' no prizes this time," said Pete. "Don't ask me."

"But what do you think it *might* be?" asked Ted.

Pete shrugged his shoulder. "Dunno, but I hear tell some one of the moneyed fellers here in town is plannin' somethin' worth while."

No matter how much Ted teased him, Pete would give no guess as to what the prize might be.

"Just you practice your ridin' and the prize can take care of itself," was all Pete would say.

"We'll start tomorrow morning," said Ted.

But Ted had forgotten that the next day was Sunday. When he woke up and saw his Sunday clothes spread out on the chair by his bed he groaned aloud.

"No riding this morning," he said.

Ted hated to dress up. His collar scratched

his neck and his suit coat pulled at his arms. He wished best clothes had never been invented.

But Sue loved to put on her Sunday dress. Her pink starched skirt and black patent-leather shoes made her feel almost grown up. When the twins met at the breakfast table, one was smiling and the other was frowning. Robby was already sitting in his high chair with a huge bib covering his Sunday suit.

"Wobby all keen," he announced, waving his egg spoon.

"You won't be clean long if you don't watch out with that spoon," said Ted, pulling at his collar. "Do we *have* to go to church today?"

Mother didn't even answer that question. She just said, "After breakfast you and Sue be careful. Don't get dirty before church."

When breakfast was over, Ted and Sue, with Robby at their heels, went out to the yard. There was nothing to do. They felt strange and uncomfortable in their Sunday clothes.

"Let's go up to the clubroom," said Ted.

"And get paint all over us?" asked Sue in a shocked voice.

"Who says we're going to paint?" said Ted.
"We can— Hey!" Ted had remembered he had
forgotten to put the blue paint away. He began
to run toward the clubroom.

Sue hesitated, but only for a minute. She knew
Ted had thought of something and she wanted
to know what it was. She followed Ted with
Robby trotting busily behind her.

When she reached the clubroom she found
Ted scrabbling through the paintbox, muttering

to himself. "It's gone," he said when he saw Sue. "I left it right here and now it's gone."

"What?" asked Sue.

"The bottle of blue paint," said Ted. "I left it right here and—"

"You said that," said Sue sternly. "You've lost my blue paint."

"Someone took it, that's what," said Ted.

Before Sue could find words to tell Ted what she thought of him, she heard Robby calling from below. "Wobby coming, here Wobby!"

"Keep him out of here," said Ted hurriedly. "Let's go." He knew Sue was angry with him and was quite willing to change the subject.

Robby was already halfway up the ladder and it took some persuasion and a good deal of pulling to get him down. Once he was safely on the ground Sue was ready to talk about the blue paint again. But she had hardly begun before Mother called that it was time for church.

"Thank goodness," muttered Ted. For once he was relieved to hear that it was church time. Mother never allowed arguments on the way to church. He was saved for a while.

The church was in the village and Daddy drove them there in the car. No one talked during the drive. The twins sat on the back seat and thought about the blue paint. Robby sat between them hugging his blanket.

"He can't take that rag into church," said Ted, as they got out of the car.

"I'll fix it," said Daddy. He took Robby's hand as they walked across the church lawn. When Robby was busy watching the people going into church, Ted saw Daddy take the blanket and put it in his hat. The hat was hung on the row of pegs in the vestibule. Then the whole family walked sedately to their pew.

Ted and Sue sat in the middle of the pew with Robby between them. Mother and Daddy sat at either end. Ted looked at the people in the seats ahead of them. He saw a fly walking up the back of old Judge Pemberley's coat. The Judge's head was nodding forward.

Ted hoped the fly would crawl up on his neck. But the fly only sat on the Judge's collar and cleaned his wings. Ted was disgusted with the fly.

Sue looked at the minister's wife and wondered when she would be allowed to wear a hat with a blue feather in it. She wished it were time to sing a hymn. Sue loved to sing. But the man who pumped the organ was sitting behind his little red curtain with his hands folded. It wasn't time to sing yet. Sue folded her hands and listened hard to the minister.

At last the organ began to hum and Sue sighed happily. "Fight the Good Fight" was one of her favorite hymns. You could sing it as loud as you wanted.

Right in the middle of the last verse, Ted jabbed Sue with his elbow. She glared at him. Ted was holding his hymn book in front of his face and whispering something. Sue leaned toward him.

"Where's Robby?" asked Ted from behind the book.

Sue looked down. The seat between them was empty. She looked on the floor. Robby wasn't there. Sue lifted her eyebrows at Ted to tell him she couldn't find Robby.

The hymn came to an end, and everyone sat

down. The church was very quiet. Then Sue heard a murmuring sound behind her. It was as though people were surprised at something and trying not to show it. She looked around quickly.

Four rows back she saw the people in the pew looking down at their feet. Then the people in the third row jumped, looked startled and bent down toward the floor. The same thing happened in the second row.

A minute later there was a sound under their own pew. Ted and Sue leaned down. Robby's head appeared from under the seat. Then all of Robby came into sight. His face was smeared with dust and his Sunday suit was streaked with dirt. But Robby was smiling. He had his blanket in one hand.

"Wobby's banka," he announced out loud. He climbed up between the twins. Then he patted his blanket into a roll, put it on the seat and lay down with his head on the blanket. His feet rested on Ted's lap.

Sue held her breath. She was afraid she might laugh right out loud. She knew what Robby had done. He had crawled to the back of the church through the open space under the pews to get his blanket.

Then Sue heard Ted gasp. She looked at him quickly. Ted was staring down at Robby's shoes. He pointed at the sole of one shoe with a shaky finger.

Sue bent forward. A few grains of dry blue paint were stuck fast on the heel of Robby's shoe. She looked at Ted with wide, wondering eyes. He looked back at her. Neither could say a word.

Both Ted and Sue stared down at Robby. He was fast asleep with his head on his blanket. His cheeks were pink, his bright curls shone. He looked like a sleeping angel.

6 *Come to the Fair*

I T WAS the longest church service Ted and
Sue had ever known. They were sure the
minister would never stop talking. Every two
minutes they leaned down and studied the telltale specks of blue paint on Robby's shoes. Then
they would look hard at Robby and wonder
whether to be angry with him or just surprised.

Robby smiled in his sleep. He didn't know
what was in store for him when he woke up.

At last the final hymn was announced. Ted
and Sue almost shouted the words. It was such

a relief to be able to do something besides sit still and be quiet. Robby stood between them, holding a hymn book upside down in both hands. He sang too, but it was his own private song. Sometimes he was still singing at the end of a verse.

The instant they were outside the church Ted and Sue turned on Robby.

"Look!" said Ted. He lifted one of Robby's feet and pointed to the paint. "Paint, Robby. Where did you get it?"

Robby inspected his shoe with great interest. "Wobby shoes," he said and patted them fondly. "Nice shoes."

"Don't bully him," said Sue. She knelt down beside him and put her hands on his shoulders. "Look here, Robby," she said gently, "did Robby take Sue's paint?"

Robby tried to stuff his blanket in his mouth.

Sue shook him, but not very gently. "Come on, Robby, tell me—"

But Sue got no further. Suddenly she felt Ted's hand on her foot. He lifted it up and almost dumped Sue on her face.

"Look out!" she shouted in a very un-Sunday voice.

"Children, quiet!" said Mother. "Remember where—"

But Ted couldn't wait for Mother to finish. "Look at your shoes!" he cried. "Lookit, lookit!" His voice cracked with excitement.

Sue did as she was told. There on the soles of both shoes were specks of blue paint. She blinked and looked again. There was no mistake. There was paint on her shoes too.

She saw Ted glaring at her. In one second he would tell her what he thought of her. So Sue said the first thing that came into her head.

"Why don't you look at your own shoes?"

Ted did as he was told, just to satisfy Sue. Then it was his turn to be astonished. There was blue paint on his shoes, too. Quite a lot of it in fact.

The twins looked at each other with round eyes. Then Sue began to giggle. Ted had to laugh too.

"Some detectives we are," he said.

"And think what awful things we were thinking about Robby!" cried Sue. She hugged Robby hard. "We thought he took all the things."

"Wobby took," said Robby, returning Sue's hug with interest.

"No, you didn't," said Sue.

"Never mind Robby," said Ted. "What I'd like to know is how we got the paint on our shoes."

They talked about it all the way home, but the more they discussed the mystery, the darker it became.

"One thing is sure," said Ted, as they drove into the yard, "whoever took the paint spilled some and we all stepped in it."

Sue nodded. "But where did they spill it?"

The twins found the answer to that question

almost immediately. At the bottom of the ladder in the shed was a thin scattering of blue paint. Clearly outlined in the patch of paint were three sets of footsteps. They knew now how the paint got on their shoes.

"We stepped in it just before church. We must have," said Ted. "We were all out here, even Robby."

Sue started to speak, but Ted waved at her to keep quiet. "I'm thinking," he said. "That paint must have been taken sometime after I went to the cow barn and this morning before church. We can pin down the time at least."

"It took a lot of brains to figure that out," said Sue, who didn't like the superior tone Ted was using. She gave her starched pink skirts a swish and walked away to the house. "I'm going to change my clothes and get ready to practice with Twinkle after dinner," she called over her shoulder.

"I claim first turn to ride," cried Ted, running after her.

But Sue knew enough not to start that argument again. Maybe Pete would think of a way.

Pete took care of the problem in very short order.

"Ladies first," he said, when Ted and Sue appeared in the barn after dinner.

Ted gave a mighty groan, but Pete paid no attention. He helped saddle Twinkle and told them what to expect on the day of the fair.

"I kind of suspect the judges will want the ponies to ride up and down that piece of road in front of the Grange Hall," he said. "You know what I mean?"

The twins nodded. They knew the fair was to be held at the Grange grounds and they knew the stretch of road Pete was talking about. It ran between the hall and an open field where the fair tents would be pitched.

"Now listen tight," said Pete. "All the ridin' exhibitions I ever seen in my time you've got to show your horse's paces. Get it?"

Ted nodded and Sue shook her head.

"Like this," said Pete. "You got to make him walk, trot, and gallop on signal. We've got to practice making Twinkle change pace just by a touch of your heel."

Sue looked at Twinkle and remembered how he liked to have his own way. She didn't think a touch of her heel would make him do what he didn't want to do.

"You try first, Sue," said Pete. "We'll make out the barnyard is that piece of road."

Ted watched Sue mount Twinkle. "If we had a decent saddle, we might have a chance," he muttered. "What other ponies are going to be at the fair, Pete?"

"There's two others in town," said Pete. "That little black one belonging to Susie Buxton and Tommy Hedden's pinto. Good ponies, too."

"And real saddles, I bet," said Ted.

" 'Tisn't the saddle, it's the ridin' that counts," said Pete. "Ready, Sue?"

Sue was ready, but she had reckoned without Robby. He had been watching quietly until now, but when Sue picked up the reins he spoke. "Wobby wide," he announced firmly.

Sue looked at Pete. They both knew what would happen if Robby didn't have a short ride. Robby was apt to use his voice loud and long when he wanted something.

"Just a little ride, Robby," said Sue and slid to the ground.

Ted snorted. "Of all the spoiled kids," he began.

But Pete silenced him with a look. "It'll save time, believe me," he said. "I can show you what I mean anyway. Just you watch me and Robby."

Pete led Twinkle up and down the yard. He showed Robby how to kick his heels against Twinkle's sides to make him change from a walk to a trot, then to a gallop.

Robby's short legs made hard work of it, but

he managed to let Twinkle know what he meant. When Twinkle galloped Robby bounced in the saddle like a cork on the waves. But he hung on.

"Thata boy!" shouted Pete, as Robby kicked Twinkle down to a walk. "You're doin' fine. Sue's turn."

The twins spent most of the afternoon with Twinkle. Pete stayed with them every minute. No matter how many mistakes they made or how cross they sometimes were with Twinkle, Pete never got impatient. He sat on the barnyard wall and told them what to do and how to manage Twinkle.

By the end of the afternoon they had learned a lot. So had Twinkle.

"Nice for a start," said Pete. "Time to give Twinkle a rest. You go do a little detecting."

Ted and Sue glanced at each other. The detective work was supposed to be a secret. It was just like Pete to know all about it.

The next few days they had little time for anything but practicing with Twinkle. Even Robby had his share of riding. The twins had learned that the best way to keep Robby quiet was to give him a short turn on Twinkle before they began their serious practice work.

"He's getting almost as good as we are," said Sue. It was the day before the fair and they were having a last trial with Twinkle. "Twinkle likes to have Robby ride him."

"His kicks ain't so troublesome as some," said Pete, looking at Ted, who sometimes kicked Twinkle rather briskly when he didn't obey right away.

Ted gazed at the pigeons on the barn roof.

"I've got a surprise for you," said Pete, who knew when he had said enough.

They crowded around Pete, who stood near Twinkle's head. Pete tapped Twinkle's neck. "Take a bow," he said in a loud voice.

Twinkle bowed his head almost to the ground. Then he lifted his right forefoot as though he wanted to shake hands.

Ted and Sue shouted with glee.

"How'd you teach him?" asked Ted, when he had shaken hands with Twinkle.

"That's a smart pony," said Pete. "I taught him off and on. Now when the exhibition's over and you line up in front of the judges, just you touch Twinkle's neck and he'll take a bow. No harm in givin' the judges the right kind of howdy-do."

"I bet none of the other ponies can do tricks," said Ted. "Now if we had a decent saddle we might have a chance."

"Never mind the saddle," said Pete. "Tomorrow morning we'll give Twinkle a good polishing, so's to be ready to start by ten o'clock. You better take the cart."

"And Jemima," said Sue with a sigh. "Twinkle won't go without her."

Sue was right. The next morning when the brushed and curried Twinkle was hitched to the cart he refused to move until Pete lifted Jemima into the cart.

"I'm gettin' a clutch of duck eggs for this bird," said Pete, fighting to hold the squawking Jemima. "I'll buy some at the fair and make her happy."

But the twins weren't interested in Jemima's troubles. Their faces were pale with excitement. Ted's hands shook as he held the reins.

"All set?" asked Pete, when he had handed

Jemima to Robby. "I'm comin' in the car with your ma and pa. We'll bring the saddle. See you there."

Pete sounded very casual. You would never know that anything unusual was about to happen.

"When are we going to draw lots?" cried Ted, as Twinkle moved forward.

"Plenty of time," said Pete. "I'm readyin' the straws."

The twins didn't talk much on the way to the fair. They were too busy thinking about who might get the longest straw. Robby held tight to

Jemima and talked to her. But their conversation was not the kind everyone could understand.

"I wonder what time the riding exhibition starts," said Sue, as they came near the fair grounds.

"Pete thinks about noon," said Ted. "Hey, listen! You can hear the music."

The sharp sound of a calliope came from somewhere ahead. Ted clucked impatiently at Twinkle. They rounded a turn in the road and all the color and noise of the fair burst into view.

Crowds of people swarmed around the tents, booths, and stands on the grounds. Everyone seemed to be talking; the voices made a great humming sound. Flags and banners waved overhead.

"Whew!" cried Sue to relieve her feelings. "It's a real fair."

"What did you expect?" demanded Ted. "There's Pete under that tree over there."

Pete signaled that they were to bring Twinkle to a small cleared area which had been fenced in for the ponies. The black pony and the pinto were already saddled. Susie Buxton and Tommy

Hedden stood by their ponies and looked at Ted and Sue. The twins looked back at them. They didn't say anything.

Ted saw that the other ponies had real leather saddles. He hated to look at the felt pad as Pete saddled Twinkle. Susie and Tommy were both much younger than the twins. It was a disgrace, thought Ted, to have to use a beginner's saddle.

"How long?" asked Ted when Twinkle was ready.

"Not long," said Pete. "See over there?" He pointed to the stretch of road in front of the Grange Hall. "Them three men are the judges."

The twins stared at the three important-looking men standing before the building. They had papers in their hands and whispered together behind their hands.

Suddenly Ted's eyes bulged. Right beside the judges, lying on the ground at their feet, was a saddle. It was a western saddle with real stirrups and a high cantle.

"L-look!" Ted grabbed Sue's arm and pointed. "Do you think—" He couldn't finish his question. He just looked at Pete.

Pete was grinning. "That's it," he said. "That's the prize."

Before the twins could say a word a loud voice boomed above the noise of the crowd. The hum of voices quieted. Everyone looked at the three judges. One of them held a megaphone.

"The draw! We've got to draw lots!" said Ted in a fierce whisper.

Pete held out his hand. Two straws showed between his fingers. Just as Ted and Sue reached out, the man with the megaphone began to speak.

"Pony riding exhibition!" he shouted. "Contenders line up before the judges."

He paused and the noisy hum of voices began again.

"Just a minute!" bellowed the man. "Quiet, please! There's just one rule about the riders. They must be under eight years of age."

7 *Ride Away, Ride Away!*

FOR one horrible second Ted was sure he was going to cry. There lay that western saddle right at the judges' feet. For a brief and glorious moment he had hoped it might belong to Twinkle. He swallowed hard and stared at the ground.

Sue didn't believe she had heard correctly. It couldn't be true. Either she or Ted had to ride Twinkle.

"He's fooling, isn't he?" she asked Pete in a small voice.

"Nope," said Pete. Pete looked surprised, too.

It was plain that he had known nothing about the rule for the riders.

Susie and Tommy mounted their ponies and walked them toward the Grange Hall. They were both under eight. They didn't have to worry. One of them would win the western saddle.

"And they've got real saddles already!" cried Ted. He couldn't help sounding angry. The disappointment was too much to bear.

Suddenly Pete snapped his fingers. "I got it!" he announced.

Ted and Sue stared at Pete. It didn't seem possible that he had thought of a way out of this terrible trouble.

Pete pointed toward the cart. The twins looked at it. They didn't see anything but Robby sitting there, holding Jemima and his blanket.

"What about it?" asked Ted.

"Robby can ride Twinkle," said Pete solemnly.

"Robby!" cried Ted and Sue both at once.

Robby smiled and nodded at them. "Wobby here," he said.

"It's your only hope," said Pete.

Ted groaned. "Good-by, saddle," he said.

But Sue ran to the cart. "Robby ride Twinkle," she said. "Robby ride now."

"He'll never do it," cried Ted. "He'll be too scared."

But Robby was delighted with the idea. He climbed out of the cart, carrying Jemima and his blanket with him. He didn't mind when Ted took the squawking Jemima from him, but he wouldn't let Sue have his blanket.

"Banka wide," he said firmly.

Sue knew enough not to argue. She folded the blanket into a neat bundle and put it on the saddle. "Sit on it," she said, beckoning to Robby.

"Good night!" shouted Ted. "That old rag will ruin everything."

"Leave him be," said Pete, as he lifted Robby into the saddle. "Just you take Jemima out to the end of the ridin' course and hold her where Twinkle can see her. It'll kind of encourage him."

Ted did as he was told. He had given up all hope of Twinkle's winning the saddle, but he wanted to help Robby all he could. He pushed his way through the crowd and stood at the end of the course holding Jemima in both hands.

Pete led Twinkle to a place beside the other two ponies. Sue trailed behind, hoping Robby wouldn't be scared at the last minute and refuse to ride. But Robby didn't mind the people crowding about or the remarks they made.

"Look at that baby on the pony," said one voice.

"He'll fall," said another.

"Isn't he cute?" said several people.

Sue agreed with the last remark. Robby's feet stuck almost straight out on either side of the saddle, but his hands held the reins firmly. He smiled at the people nearest him.

"Now listen, Robby," said Pete, when Twinkle stood beside the other ponies, "just you ride like we did at home. See Jemima down there?" He pointed at Ted and Jemima.

Robby nodded. "Wobby wide," he said. "Go see quack-quack."

"That's right," said Sue. "Just do—"

But the announcer's voice cut her off short. "First pony ridden by Susie Buxton."

Susie started off down the open road. The way was lined with people who pressed forward to watch. The black pony didn't like so many curious faces. He shied several times and refused to move out of a walk. Susie's face got red and she cried a little. But everyone cheered her just the same.

Tommy Hedden came next. The pinto felt very frisky. He danced down the roadway, just as though he was showing off. Sometimes he trotted, sometimes he galloped. Tommy was out of breath from pulling the reins when he came back to the judges' stand. The crowd cheered heartily.

"Last entry!" shouted the announcer loudly.

"Your turn, Robby," whispered Sue. "Ride, Robby, ride!"

Robby kicked his heels against Twinkle. "Go, pony, do!" he commanded.

Twinkle obeyed. He walked forward with sedate steps. He went straight for the spot where Ted and Jemima were.

Ted was so nervous he began to shout. "Kick him again, Robby!" he yelled and waved Jemima in the air.

Jemima didn't like such airy treatment and said so in a series of angry quacks.

But Robby heard Ted and did as he was told. Now Twinkle was trotting briskly. Robby bobbed up and down in the saddle, but he hung on.

The crowd cheered. They yelled louder than they had for the other two ponies. Ted noticed it and a great wild hope grew within him.

"Kick him again, Robby!" he bellowed and once more waved Jemima overhead.

This time Jemima had had enough. She pecked Ted's hand so hard he had to notice her. As he grabbed at her flapping wings he saw a

patch of blue on her breast feathers. Blue—blue
paint. The thought flickered through his mind.
But he couldn't think about it now. A great
shout from the crowd made Ted forget Jemima
entirely.

Robby was galloping now, coming straight
toward Ted and Jemima. Twinkle's feet pounded
the ground, his mane and tail flew in the wind.
Robby clung to the saddle with both hands. He
wasn't sitting on it at all. He didn't have a chance
to sit anywhere just now. Behind him streamed
the blanket, a tattered banner in the breeze.

"Whoa, Twinkle, whoa!" cried Ted, as
Twinkle bore down upon him. "Kick him,
Robby, kick him!"

Robby couldn't kick. His feet weren't anywhere near Twinkle. But Twinkle knew what to
do without any signal. He slowed to a trot, then
to a walk, and stopped right in front of Ted. He
neighed softly to Jemima.

But Jemima quacked crossly. She sounded
as though she were telling Twinkle what she
thought of Ted.

"Be quiet," said Ted to Jemima. "Robby, you

take Twinkle over there." He pointed to the judges' stand.

Before Robby could obey, Twinkle turned and walked back to join the other two ponies. Then Ted knew that Twinkle was in charge. He knew exactly what he was supposed to do.

Suddenly the people were quiet. Everyone watched the three judges as they whispered together. Ted and Sue watched hardest of all. Sometimes the judges looked at the ponies, then wrote things on pieces of paper. It was the longest few minutes Ted and Sue had ever known.

Ted and Sue watched Robby, too. He was holding his blanket under one arm. He was also sucking his thumb. He didn't look as though he cared about anything but a nap.

Suddenly one of the judges stepped forward. In one hand he held a blue ribbon. He seemed to be trying to make up his mind which pony to give it to.

At that moment Ted remembered that Twinkle knew how to bow and shake hands. He longed to shout to Robby and remind him to pat Twinkle's neck, but he didn't dare. If only Robby would stop sucking his thumb and pat Twinkle.

But Ted had forgotten that Twinkle was wide awake. When the judge paused in front of him, Twinkle lowered his head in a polite bow. He raised his right forefoot and waited.

The crowd gave a great cheer as the judge

leaned down to take Twinkle's hoof. The cheers
were even louder when the judge pinned the
blue ribbon on Twinkle's bridle. The noise was
tremendous. It was like a sea of sound breaking
over Ted. He couldn't shout. He was too happy.

Sue was crying. She couldn't help it. It was
almost too wonderful to believe. Twinkle had
won the blue ribbon. He had won the saddle

too. She saw the judge trying to hand it to Robby. But Robby just stared at it.

Ted and Sue managed the saddle between them. Trying to hold Jemima and the saddle too was almost too much for Ted. Sue wanted to hug the saddle and Robby both at once. Mother and Daddy and Pete were beside them. Everyone talked, everyone laughed, and they all hugged Robby.

Somehow they got away from the crowding, pushing people to the open space beneath the tree. They all carried something. Ted held the saddle. Sue had Jemima. Pete carried Robby on his shoulders.

"Nice goin', old feller," said Pete, as he put Robby in the cart.

Robby didn't answer. He lay down on the seat and stuffed his blanket under his head. He was ready for a nap.

"Twinkle was wonderful, too," said Sue. "He shook hands all by himself." She tried to hug Twinkle, but Jemima flapped her wings so hard Sue had to use both hands to hold her.

"That duck," said Ted. "Say, there was something about her. Something funny." He frowned as he tried to remember. But he didn't bother to think about Jemima for long. It was more fun to inspect the western saddle. It was a beautiful saddle, better than any saddle he had ever imagined. Best of all it belonged to him. At least it was partly Sue's and partly Robby's, too.

After the excitement of the riding exhibition the rest of the fair seemed almost tame to the twins. By midafternoon they were ready to go home.

"Let's get out of here," said Ted. "I want to try the saddle."

"The others have already left," said Sue.

"I wish they'd taken that duck," said Ted. "She's still sitting in the cart as though she owned it. Did Pete get the duck eggs for her?"

Sue nodded. "He's going to give them to Jemima and let her hatch some ducklings." She lifted Jemima from the seat to make more room.

Jemima flapped her wings furiously when Sue touched her.

"Look at that blue spot on her feathers," said Sue. "How did it get there?"

Robby stared, sucking his thumb.

Ted peered at Jemima. He wrinkled his forehead as he stared at the patch of blue on her breast feathers. He had noticed that spot before and it had made him think of something. Now he couldn't remember what it was.

"It's funny," he said, as he took up the reins, "that spot reminded me of something, but I—" He stopped and stared at Sue. "Good night!"

Suddenly he knew what that patch of blue meant. He dropped the reins and snatched up the startled Jemima. In spite of her protesting squawks he held her tight to get a better view of that telltale smudge of blue.

"What are you doing?" demanded Sue, grabbing the reins.

"Look at that!" said Ted. He thrust Jemima right in Sue's face. "Don't you get it?"

"No," said Sue, "and take that duck out of my eyes. I'm trying to drive."

Ted dumped Jemima back on the seat next

to Robby. "Just wait till Pete hears about this. He won't talk so much about my being a detective after this. Here, let me drive. We've got to get home."

Sue knew Ted had another remarkable idea. Somehow it was connected with their detective work and the patch of blue on Jemima's feathers. She wished she knew what it all meant. Perhaps if she pretended she did, Ted would tell her.

"Jemima must have gotten the blue paint on her just the way we did on our shoes," she said. "But I never saw her near the shed."

Ted grinned in a maddening way. "She hasn't been in the shed," he said.

That was all he would say. All the way home Sue made little remarks, pretending she knew what Ted was thinking about. But Ted just shook his head and looked mysterious. He didn't say a word.

By the time Twinkle turned into the driveway Sue was almost beside herself with curiosity. Pete was waiting for them in the barn door, holding the new saddle, which he had brought home in the car.

"Here it is," said Pete, holding the saddle toward Ted. "Suppose you want to try it right off."

But Ted didn't seem to hear Pete. He was out of the cart before it stopped. So was Jemima. With a mighty flap of her wings, she leaped from the cart and headed for Twinkle's stall. She and Ted reached the manger at the same moment. A fury of quacks and shouts burst forth.

"No, you don't!" cried Ted. "Out of the way! *Ouch!*"

"Quack, quack, quack!" shouted Jemima, pecking smartly at any part of Ted she could reach.

"What in tarnation's going on?" demanded Pete. He headed for the stall with Robby and Sue at his heels.

They found Ted leaning into the manger with Jemima perched on his back, pecking diligently at his head.

"Get that duck off me!" cried Ted.

Pete grabbed Jemima and held her firmly under one arm. "What's going on in there?" asked Pete. "You gone crazy?"

Ted didn't answer. He was scratching through the hay at the back of the manger. Suddenly he gave a shout of triumph. "I found them! They're here! I knew it! I guessed right!"

Something hard landed at Sue's feet. She looked down and saw her diamond doorknob lying in the straw. She blinked and looked again. There it was, her precious doorknob that she had never hoped to see again. She dived at it and held it tight in both hands.

Ted was tossing more things from the manger now. Pete's cowbell fell with a tinkling sound,

Ted's piece of quartz with a thud. Last of all the bottle of blue paint hit the straw.

Pete and Sue were too surprised to say anything. But Robby and Jemima had plenty to say. Jemima said it with furious squawks and Robby in a bellow of rage.

"Yeggs! Mine yeggs!" he roared. "Quack's wound yeggs!" He tried to pick up the things, but Ted got them first.

"No, you don't," said Ted. "Leave them alone."

Robby was sobbing now. Between his sobs he repeated the word "yeggs" over and over again.

Pete let Jemima go and she flopped angrily

into the manger. They watched her scratch through the hay, quacking in a disappointed way.

"Well, I'll be switched," said Pete in a wondering voice. "So Jemima had them all along. How in—" He stopped and looked down at Robby, who was sitting in the straw with his blanket over his face to smother his sobs.

Suddenly Pete snapped his fingers. "I got it!" he cried.

"I haven't," said Sue. "Who put those things in the manger?"

Pete and Ted didn't answer in words. They just pointed at Robby.

Sue's eyes opened wide. "Robby! He wouldn't, he couldn't!"

"Sure," said Ted, who was aching to tell the story. "Robby gave all those things to Jemima. It was the paint off the bottle on her feathers that gave her away. She's been sitting on them, but I don't see why."

"She's settin'," said Pete. "I told you that before. Don't you remember how Robby took the eggs from the settin' hen in the grain room?

That's what gave him the idea Jemima might want some eggs too."

"Yeggs," moaned Robby. "Wound yeggs."

"Yeggs is right," said Pete. "He musta set out to collect anything as near round like an egg as he could find."

"I said so," cried Ted. "Remember, Sue, when we painted the sign, how I said all the lost things were round?"

Sue still couldn't believe Robby had done it. "I don't think Robby took the things," she said stoutly.

"Wobby did," said Robby between sobs.

Sue had to believe it then. She leaned down and hugged Robby. "He didn't mean to," she said. "He was just trying to make Jemima happy."

"I know what'll make her happier," said Pete. He brought the box of duck eggs and slipped them one by one under Jemima.

Jemima settled down on the eggs with a pleased quack. She looked at the row of faces peering down at her.

"Quack," said Jemima in a commanding way.

It was just as if she had said, "Go away and don't bother me."

"All right, sister," said Pete. He led the way out of the stall. Then he put a hand on Ted's shoulder. "Good work, feller. You're a detective right enough."

Ted tried not to look too pleased. "It wasn't anything," he said. "I just happened to notice the paint on Jemima and—well, the rest was easy."

"I don't think it was easy at all," said Sue, looking admiringly at Ted.

"Girls aren't detectives," said Ted.

Sue's face got a little red. She was about to argue the point when Pete interrupted.

"How about trying the new saddle," he said.

"I claim to use it first," cried Ted.

"No, me!" said Sue.

They looked at each other. Then both at once they looked at Robby. He still sat in the stall with his blanket over his face. But his sobs were not so loud now.

Ted and Sue remembered Robby at the fair. They remembered how he looked galloping down the road on Twinkle's back, his feet high in the air. Robby had won the blue ribbon for them and the western saddle.

Then they both spoke at the same time. "Let Robby," they said.

Pete grinned. "That's the way we say it," said Pete.